For Aunt J.

Neal Porter Books

Text copyright © 2019 by Philip C. Stead

Illustrations copyright © 2019 by Erin E. Stead

All Rights Reserved

HOLIDAY HOUSE is registered in the U.S. Patent and Trademark Office.

Printed and bound in July 2018 at Hong Kong Graphics Ltd., China.

The artwork was made with mono printed oil inks, colored pencils, and graphite.

www.holidayhouse.com

First Edition

10 9 8 7 6 5 4 3 2 1

Library of Congress Cataloging-in-Publication Data is available.

ISBN: 978-0-8234-4160-0 (hardcover)

Music for Mister Moon

Written by PHILIP C. STEAD
Illustrated by ERIN E. STEAD

NEAL PORTER BOOKS
HOLIDAY HOUSE / NEW YORK

WHEN HARRIET HENRY came down for dinner her parents said, "Someday you will play your cello in a big orchestra. Won't that make you happy?"

Harriet imagined crowds of people all dressed up like penguins. Her hands became sweaty and her face became hot. "No," she said with a sigh. "I don't think that will make me happy." Harriet pushed her green beans into a neat row.

Then she closed her eyes and changed her parents into penguins.
"May I excuse myself, please?" she asked.

Harriet Henry did not want to play in a big orchestra. Harriet Henry
wanted to play her cello alone.

When Harriet was alone she would change her room into a little house with a kitchen table, a chair, a teacup, and a fireplace.

And when everything was quiet and still she would draw her bow,

and—

HOO-HOO-HOOOOOOOO!

Harriet peeked her head out the window. "Please, go away," she said.
"I want to be alone." Then she sat back down, drew her bow,

and—

HOO-HOO-HOOOOOOOO!

Harriet took her teacup and threw it out the window.
Hoo? asked the owl, and he flew off into the night.

Harriet did not want to hurt the owl. *I just want to be alone*, she thought. Then she sat back down and tried to change her regret into a new teacup. But before she could, Harriet's little house filled up with smoke. Quickly she made herself a bucket, filled it with water, and tossed it onto the fire. Then she ran outside.

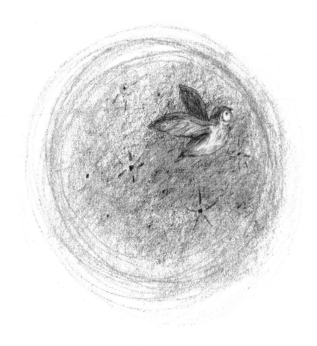

"Hello?" came a voice.

Harriet looked up and saw the moon. "Why are you sitting in my chimney?" she asked.

"Because I am stuck," said the moon.

"Why are you stuck?" asked Harriet.

"Because," said the moon, "you hit me with your teacup, and I fell from the sky."

Harriet felt horrible. "I am really sorry," she said. Then she made herself a ladder, climbed up to the roof, and pulled the moon out of her chimney.

"My name is Harriet Henry," said Harriet. "But you can call me Hank."

"I am the moon," said the moon. "But you can call me Mister Moon."

"Do you get chilly up in the sky?" asked Hank.

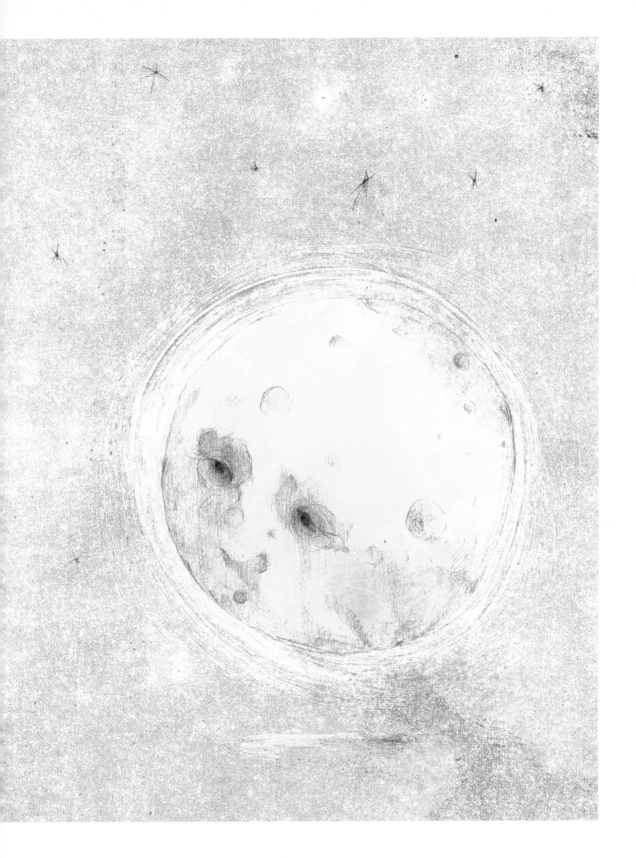

"Yes," said Mister Moon. "I do."

"When I am chilly," said Hank, "I wear a warm hat."

Then Hank made herself a wagon. She pulled Mister Moon through
the neighborhood, past the lake and the broken street lamp, all the way
to the hatmaker.

"Mister Moon would like a hat," said Hank. She pulled a dollar from
her pocket.
"Mister Moon may have any hat he likes," said the hatmaker. Then
he gave Hank back her dollar because once, when he was very young,
he had fallen in love on a moonlit night.

Mister Moon chose the striped hat.

"Do you like being the moon?" asked Hank.

"Yes," said Mister Moon. "But sometimes I wish I wasn't the moon."

Hank stopped at the broken street lamp. "What would you do if you weren't the moon?" she asked.

Mister Moon glowed brightly on the sidewalk below. "I would row in a boat," he answered with a soft smile. "Every night I watch my reflection float from one side of the lake to the other. Just once I'd like to float on the lake for real."

Hank pulled Mister Moon to the edge of the lake. "You wait here," she said. Then she went to knock on the fisherman's door.

"Mister Moon would like to row in a boat," said Hank. She pulled a dollar from her pocket.

"Mister Moon may borrow any boat he likes," said the fisherman. Then he gave Hank back her dollar because once, long ago, the moon had chased away a storm and guided him safely home.

Mister Moon chose the red boat.

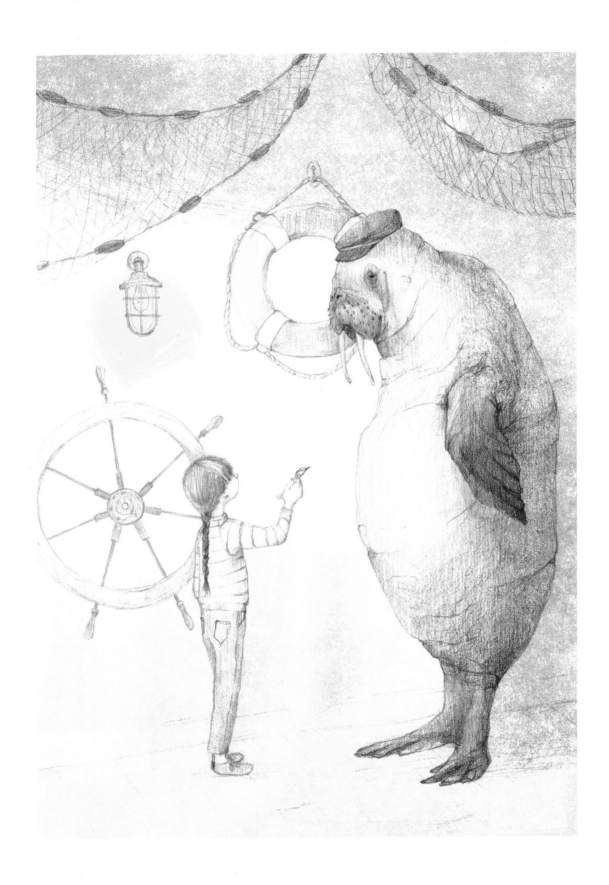

Hank and Mister Moon rowed to the middle of the lake.

"This is nice," said Hank.

"Yes, this is nice," said Mister Moon. "I like the sound of the water

when it drips from the oars. And I like the sound of the buoy bell
coming from far away. I think you are lucky," said Mister Moon.
"There is so much music down below. It is so quiet up in the sky."

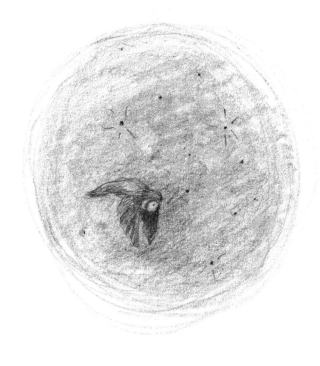

"I think it is time for me to go back home," said Mister Moon. He cast his cool light across the water without a sound. "Will you come, too, and play your cello for me?"

Hank's hands became sweaty and her face became hot. "I do not like to play for crowds," she said. "But maybe if you close your eyes and promise not to cheer."

"I promise," said Mister Moon.

Hank rowed back to the dock. "You wait here," she said.

Then she pulled her wagon back to the fisherman. "May I borrow your net, please?"

And she pulled her wagon back to the hatmaker. "May I have another hat, please?"

Last, she pulled her wagon back to the owl. "I am sorry that I scared you before. Will you help me to return Mister Moon?"

"I will," said the owl. "Because every owl is a friend of the moon."

Then the owl collected every owl.

Hank collected her cello.

And together they collected Mister Moon

and brought him back home.

"Thank you, owls," said Hank.
And then, when everything was quiet and still, Hank drew her bow
and played her music for no one but Mister Moon.